A Note to Parents

For many children, learning math is difficult and "I hate math!" is their first response — to which many parents silently add "Me, too!" Children often see adults comfortably reading and writing, but they rarely have such models for mathematics. And math fear can be catching!

The easy-to-read stories in this **Hello Math** series were written to give children a positive introduction to mathematics and parents a pleasurable re-acquaintance with a subject that is important to everyone's life. **Hello Math** stories make mathematical ideas accessible, interesting, and fun for children. The activities and suggestions at the end of each book provide parents with a hands-on approach to help children develop mathematical interest and confidence.

Enjoy the mathematics!
• Give your child a chance to retell the story. The more familiar children are with the story, the more they will understand its mathematical concepts.
• Use the colorful illustrations to help children "hear and see" the math at work in the story.
• Treat the math activities as games to be played for fun. Follow your child's lead. Spend time on those activities that engage your child's interest and curiosity.
• Activities, especially ones using physical materials, help make abstract mathematical ideas concrete.

Learning is a messy process and learning about math calls for children to become immersed in lively experiences that help them make sense of mathematical concepts and symbols.

Although learning about numbers is basic to math, other ideas, such as identifying shapes and patterns, measuring, collecting and interpreting data, reasoning logically, and thinking about chance are also important. By reading these stories and having fun with the activities, you'll help your child enthusiastically say "*Hello, Math*," instead of "I hate math."

—Marilyn Burns
National Mathematics Educator
Author of *The I Hate Mathematics! Book*

For Jeffrey Wayland
— B.L.

Copyright © 1997 by Scholastic Inc.
The activities on pages 29-32 copyright ©1997 by Marilyn Burns.
All rights reserved. Published by Scholastic Inc.
CARTWHEEL BOOKS and the CARTWHEEL BOOKS logo
are registered trademarks of Scholastic Inc.
HELLO MATH READER and the HELLO MATH READER logo
are trademarks of Scholastic Inc.

Library of Congress Cataloging-in-Publication Data

Ling, Bettina.
The fattest, tallest, biggest snowman ever / by Bettina Ling; illustrated by Michael Rex.
p.   cm. — (Hello math reader. Level 3)
Summary: Two children use non-standard measurements, such as paper clips, sticks, and their arms, to determine who has built the biggest snowman. Includes measurement activities and games.
ISBN 0-590-97284-7
[1. Measurement — Fiction.]
I. Rex, Michael, ill. II. Title. III. Series.
PZ7.L66245Fat 1997
[E] — dc20   96-20478
                                                            CIP
                                                            AC

20 19 18 17 16 15 14 13   07 08 09

Printed in the U.S.A.   23

First Scholastic printing, February 1997

THE FATTEST, TALLEST, BIGGEST SNOWMAN EVER

by Bettina Ling
Illustrated by Michael Rex
Math Activities by Marilyn Burns

Hello Math Reader — Level 3

SCHOLASTIC INC.

New York Toronto London Auckland Sydney

Jeff wanted to be the best at something.
But somehow, somebody else
was always better.

In the spring,
Annie hit longer home runs,
and Todd caught more balls.

In the summer,

Luis swam faster,

and Rhonda built a bigger sand castle.

In the fall,

Sam built a taller tree house,

and Maria made larger leaf piles.

That winter, Jeff decided he was
going to find something,
anything,
that he could do best.

"Let's have a snowball-throwing contest,"
he said to his friends one day.
Splat! Sam's snowball hit a wooden fence.

So did Rhonda's.
Annie's snowball sailed over it.
Plop! Jeff's snowball didn't even
reach the fence.

"Let's race," Jeff said to his friends
at the park the next day.

Todd hopped on his sled and took off.
Jeff and Maria shot down the hill
at the same speed.
Luis's sled flew right past them.

"I think I have to go home, now,"
said Jeff sadly.
"Wait for me," said Maria.

Jeff and Maria walked home.

"Let's build snowmen," said Jeff.

"Okay," said Maria.

*And I am going to make the biggest snowman
ever*, Jeff thought to himself.

Jeff and Maria each rolled three snowballs.

A big one,

a medium-sized one,

and a small one.

They put the snowballs on top of each other.

Then they raced back inside

to get things to use to dress their snowmen.

When they were finished,
Jeff's snowman had black button eyes,
a crayon nose,
a paper clip smile,
and a funny hat and tie.

Maria's snowman had charcoal eyes,
a carrot nose,
a raisin smile,
and a colorful hat.

"I made the biggest snowman ever!" said Jeff.

"But mine's the same size,"
said Maria.

"Mine is bigger," said Jeff.

"Maybe mine is bigger," said Maria.

"Let's measure them," Jeff said.

"How?" asked Maria.

"Let me think," said Jeff.

Jeff had an idea.

"Let's use our arms. We'll see whose snowman is the fattest."

"Yeah, but whose arms should we use?" asked Maria.

Maria and Jeff stood back-to-back.

They put out their arms.

Maria's were longer.

"You do it," Jeff said.

Maria put her arms around Jeff's snowman.
She couldn't reach.
She couldn't reach around her snowman,
either.

Jeff found some string in his pocket.

"I have another idea," he said.

But there wasn't enough string to go around
the biggest part of either snowman.

"I know!" said Jeff.

"Let's make a paper clip chain.

We can count how many paper clips

it takes to go around the biggest

part of our snowmen."

"Good idea!" Maria said.

She took the paper clip smile

off Jeff's snowman.

"Look. You already started your chain!"

Jeff and Maria measured their snowmen.
Jeff's snowman was 48 paper clips
around the bottom.
Maria's snowman was 45.

"My snowman is fatter," cried Jeff. "I have
the biggest snowman."

"Okay, your snowman is fatter," said Maria.

"But I think that my snowman is taller."

"Let's measure," said Jeff.

"How?" asked Maria.

"We can hold a branch next to our snowmen
and mark how tall they are," Jeff said.

He took a piece of charcoal
from Maria's snowman.
"We can use this to make our marks,"
Jeff said.

"Now my snowman has only one eye!"
said Maria.
"Well, my snowman doesn't have a mouth,"
said Jeff.

Jeff and Maria took turns holding the branch
next to the snowmen.

"See! My snowman is taller," said Maria.

"It's the biggest."

"Well, my snowman is fatter," said Jeff.

"It's the biggest."

"I think it's a tie," said Maria.

"A tie!" said Jeff.

"I'll never be the *best* at anything!"

The next day was sunny.

Jeff saw Maria in her front yard.

"Hey! Your snowman looks shorter,"
he called.

"No, it's not," said Maria.

"I think we measured wrong," Jeff said.

"Okay, fine. Let's do it again," said Maria.

"Your snowman looks a little thinner, anyway."

They measured again with the paper clips
and the stick.

Maria's snowman was shorter.

Jeff's snowman was thinner.

"It's still a tie," said Maria.

Jeff didn't say anything.

The next day was very sunny.
Jeff waited for Maria after
school.
He had his hands behind his
back.

"I'm going to prove my snowman
is the biggest," Jeff said.
He pulled out a tape measure
and a yardstick.

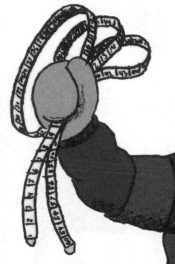

"We'll see," said Maria.

Jeff and Maria raced toward
Maria's front yard.
But when they arrived,
they got a big surprise.

No snowmen!
"The sun must have melted them," said Maria.
"Now I can't measure which snowman was
bigger," Jeff said.

"And I'll never be the best at anything."

"You're the best thinker!" said Maria.
"Whose idea was it
to have a snowball contest?
Who thought of the sled race?
Who figured out how to measure snowmen?"

"I think I see what you mean," Jeff said.
"But, I'm still going to build
the fattest, tallest, biggest snowman ever,"
he added.
"What about the sun?" Maria asked.

"We'll build snowmen in the shade!"
Jeff said.

"When it comes to ideas,
you're the best!" said Maria.

• ABOUT THE ACTIVITIES •

Measurement is an important and practical part of mathematics. We measure the length of the hallway to see if a rug will fit, a cup of flour for a recipe, children's height to check their growth, and so on. We've learned to use a variety of tools to determine the sizes of things, and to let the purpose of our measuring determine how accurate we need to be.

Most children are interested in the sizes of things, and comparing objects is their first measuring experience. They talk about things as big or little, and bigger or smaller. With more experience, however, they begin to use more specific terminology like longer or shorter, heavier or lighter, thicker or thinner, and so on.

When children can't compare two objects directly, they find something to help them measure, such as sticks, coins, blocks, paper clips, or their hands or feet. Although using these tools gives measurements that are nonstandard and imprecise, it lays the foundation for children's later learning about using standard measures and accuracy.

The activities in this section give children experience with measuring lengths of objects in different ways. Follow your child's interests, and enjoy the math!

—Marilyn Burns

You'll find tips and suggestions for guiding the activities whenever you see a box like this!

Retelling the Story

When they measured their snowmen with paper clips, Jeff's snowman was 48 paper clips around the bottom. Maria's snowman was 45. How many more paper clips did Jeff use? Make a chain of 48 paper clips and see what you can find that is just about as long.

Jeff's snowman was fatter, but Maria's snowman was taller. Maria called this a tie. Do you agree? Why or why not?

The next day, Maria's snowman was shorter. Jeff's snowman was thinner. Why was this so?

Arm Lengths

Maria tried to measure the snowmen with her arms. But she couldn't reach around. Try measuring things with your arms stretched out. How about the width of the refrigerator door? The length of your bed? The width of your bed? Around the kitchen table? The height of a kitchen chair? Around somebody's waist? Across the bathroom?

String-a-Long Game

Jeff tried to measure the snowmen with string. It was a good idea, but Jeff's string wasn't long enough to go around. You can try measuring with string, too.

To play this game, you need a ball of string, a pair of scissors, things from around the house, and a partner.

To start, put a fork on the table. Look carefully at how long it is, but don't touch it. When you're ready, cut a piece of string that you think is just about as long as the fork.

Then the other person does the same. Remember, no touching!

Compare your pieces of string to the fork and see which one is closer in length.

Try the same game with other objects — cans from the kitchen cupboard, pencils, crayons, toy cars, the length of a telephone book, and on and on.

Body Measuring With Paper Clips

Jeff and Maria were able to measure around their snowmen with paper clips. Measuring with paper clips is a good idea because you can stretch them in a straight line or measure around things.

Try taking different measurements on your body with paper clips.

How many paper clips tall are you?

How many paper clips long is your arm?

How many paper clips go around your waist?

How many go around your wrist?

How many paper clips long is your foot?

How long is your pinky finger?

What else can you measure?

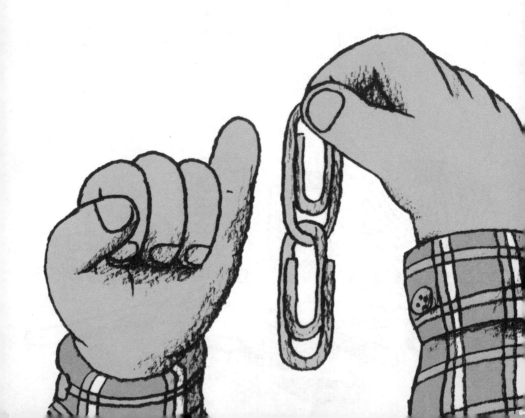